SCARE SCHOOL

Meany Screamy Dancing

Based on the original Casper animations
Adapted by Maureen Haselhurst

GW00870525

Casper's Scare School

Casper
The Friendly Ghost

Mantha
The Zombie
with Style

Ra
The Funky
Mummy

Micky and Monaco
The Hip-Hop Sisters

Alder and Dash
The Goofy Headmaster

Thatch
The Mean Dancing Machine

3

It was the day of the Meany Screamy dance contest. Everyone at Scare School was dance crazy.

The classrooms were full of groovy
spooks trying out their dance moves.

Scream! Dance Mean! Win Tickets for Grizzly Land

"Wow! The meanest dancer will win tickets for Grizzly Land," said Ra.

"I'm not very good at being mean," said Casper.

"You can learn," said Mantha. "Come on, I'll show you."

"Hi Thatch," said Micky. "Do you want us to teach you how to dance mean?"

"Get lost!" said Thatch.

"How rude!" said Micky.
"How very uncool!" agreed Monaco.

"You're a great dancer, Mantha," said Thatch. "We could make a great team."

"No way!" said Mantha. "I want to dance with Casper."

"Mean dancing isn't for silly little ghosts," said Thatch.

"He's right," said Casper sadly.
"Bye, Mantha."

So Casper went away!

At last it was night. It was time for the dance contest to begin! Scare School was full of excitement.

The headmaster, Alder and Dash, started the contest.

"Let's see you push and shove!" said Alder.

"Make sure you stamp on your partner's toes!" said Dash.

"Dance mean!" they called.

The music began to boom and everyone began to dance.

"You are not scary or mean!" said Alder.

"You are too nice to your partners!" said Dash.

"Thatch is the meanest so far," agreed Alder and Dash.

"Wait!" said Ra. "Watch me!"

Ra ran onto the dance floor with Mantha. Scare School went wild!
Ra and Mantha did all their meanest dance moves.

"Wow! Mega mean!" called Alder.
"That mummy can't beat me!"
said Thatch.

"But I might!" said a voice.

Down from the roof came the white shape of Casper.

Round and round went Casper. He
flew in circles around Thatch's head.
"Stop it! I feel dizzy!" said Thatch.

"And the winner is ... " called Alder and Dash. "Casper – the ghost with the most!"

Casper went red.

"I tried to be mean," he said, "but, sort of, friendly-mean."

"That was such a mean dance, I really wish I'd done it!" said Thatch. "But I'll win next time, Casper. Just you wait and see!"